李昌憲 著
Poems by Lee Chang-hsien

戴茉莉 譯
Translated by Emily Anna Deasy

人生茶席 ：

台灣茶詩

The Tea Session of Life ：
The poems of Taiwanese Tea

李昌憲漢英雙語詩集
Mandarin – English

台灣詩叢 • Taiwan Poetry Series 10

【總序】詩推台灣意象

叢書策劃／李魁賢

　　進入21世紀，台灣詩人更積極走向國際，個人竭盡所能，在詩人朋友熱烈參與支持下，策畫出席過印度、蒙古、古巴、智利、緬甸、孟加拉、馬其頓等國舉辦的國際詩歌節，並編輯《台灣心聲》等多種詩選在各國發行，使台灣詩人心聲透過作品傳佈國際間。接續而來的國際詩歌節邀請愈來愈多，已經有應接不暇的趨向。

　　多年來進行國際詩交流活動最困擾的問題，莫如臨時編輯帶往國外交流的選集，大都應急處理，不但時間緊迫，且選用作品難免會有不週。因此，興起策畫【台灣詩叢】雙語詩系的念頭。若台灣詩人平常就有雙語詩集出版，隨時可以應用，詩作交流與詩人交誼雙管齊下，更具實際成效，對台灣詩的國際交流活動，當更加順利。

　　以【台灣】為名，著眼點當然有鑑於台灣文學在國際間名目不彰，台灣詩人能夠有機會在國際努力開拓空間，非為個人建立知名度，而是為推展台灣意象的整體事功，期待開創台灣文學的長久景象，才能奠定寶貴的歷史意義，台灣文學終必在世界文壇上佔有地位。

　　實際經驗也明顯印證，台灣詩人參與國際詩交流活動，很受

重視，帶出去的詩選集也深受歡迎，從近年外國詩人和出版社與本人合作編譯台灣詩選，甚至主動翻譯本人詩集在各國文學雜誌或詩刊發表，進而出版外譯詩集的情況，大為增多，即可充分證明。

　　承蒙秀威資訊科技公司一本支援詩集出版初衷，慨然接受【台灣詩叢】列入編輯計畫，對台灣詩的國際交流，提供推進力量，希望能有更多各種不同外語的雙語詩集出版，形成進軍國際的集結基地。

2017.02.15誌

目次

茶詩一味

生活
從一杯茶開始

香浮動
白雲出岫
採茶風景畫
懸掛在心中
詩意正濃

時間
如禪者入定

品茶
湯甘醇
有好靈感
寫下一首詩
啊！茶詩一味

2010.4.15

品茗

下班後泡壺好茶
讓工作壓力有出口

水在茶與壺中翻轉
情緒隨茶湯順暢

一切慢慢　慢慢
慢　慢　沉　澱

品味心靈在茶中
融合為一的境界

2010.4.15

養壺

養茗壺　話乾坤
三十年真情如一

細心撫摩妳的肌膚
每一寸都是情緣

妳面色紅潤生輝
我頭髮白鶴飛雪

嘆人生甲子須臾
但求壺中日月長

2010.4.15

茶溫香溢

茶溫香溢　這時分
茶葉在壺中甦醒
籠罩茶山的雲霧
讓茶葉躲起來　釀
香氣　瞬間溢滿這空間

茶溫香溢　這時分
主客聚會　因緣牽引
愛茶人以五種感官*
品味白瓷杯中飄茶香
日日是好日的幸福

*註：眼：視覺，看茶葉製作過程完成的外觀。

耳：聽覺，聽達人說明加上自己的體會，詮釋茶湯。

鼻：嗅覺，聞茶葉是否有異味，沖泡後的聞香。

舌：味覺，甘醇、苦澀、清爽、順喉、回韻等等，依個人品味。

身：觸覺，拿茶葉輕捏，若易碎即較新鮮；泡開的茶葉，拿來看是否為手採一心兩葉，或機器採收。

以上說明只是舉例，把喝茶空間的佈置，舉凡茶席、茶器、茶葉等的品賞、品味等等當成藝術，當作修行，端視個人需求，歡喜就好。

2013.10.15

生活

退休後慢慢體會
生活因無爭而平靜
沒有工作壓力可以興起

用心感受自在幸福
自由創作後放空時刻
品茶而忘茶而靜默

2015.2.15

玉蘭茶香

聞茶香開車數百公里
入住茶農經營的民宿
位於山頭視野遼闊

遠眺豐饒的蘭陽平原
讓風來熨平蓄積的壓力
享用完特色風味晚餐
茶農請我們試新茶

彷彿從雲霧中走出來
玉蘭茶湯清亮鮮爽
在這氛圍中靜心品飲

主人乘興拿出得頭獎的
茶香撲鼻入肺
茶湯潤喉回甘

共邀蘭陽平原的萬家燈火
一起來品玉蘭茶香

2013.10.15

去貓空找鐵觀音

想嚐正宗木柵鐵觀音的滋味
十多年前女兒陪我照書上介紹
去貓空找鐵觀音比賽茶
達人親自泡剛領回的得獎茶

深琥珀色清亮的茶湯
熟果香濃得化不開
焙火味在舌尖跳舞

他說：要放一段時間
等焙火味完全退盡
這款茶滋味會更甘醇

張姓茶農的祖先從安溪渡黑水溝
把鐵觀音茶苗種在木柵地區
茶樹年年綠　貓空壺穴水長流
鐵觀音製茶技術在此代代相傳

2013.10.15

碧湖

走在茶園與竹林間
近看茶樹爭萌新芽
遠看台灣群山競高
好美的茶山風情畫

步道崎嶇　走到大尖山三角點
從天氣晴朗到烏雲密佈
只在喘息間　山雨欲來
嚇大家立即折返

真希望下一場雨消暑
陪茶樹淋雨也很幸運吧
我的思緒停留雲層之上
翻飛的詩句悠遊群山

客問：碧湖為什麼沒有湖
老闆：雲霧就是湖

就像現在看出去
是湖是海任意想像

老闆沖泡一壺自製好茶
邀大家靜下心來品茗
用一顆善感的心　疼愛
台灣好山好水好好珍惜

2013.10.15

上山製茶

親身體驗製茶
嵐氣蒸熱全身
汗水濕透全身

將茶菁均勻揉捻
解塊再揉捻
在製茶間靜置發酵

等待時間　趺坐如禪者
茶樹悄然進入我心房
雲霧也跟著進來

等到發酵程度如預期
烘乾成深褐色紅烏龍
茶在歌唱　我們用心傾聽

2015.10.15

尋紅烏龍茶記

鹿野高台春雨綿綿
厚生茶園主人細說
紅烏龍茶製程

以一心兩葉烏龍茶菁
重凋萎重攪拌
特殊的烘焙技術
留下有益人體的成分
減少咖啡因單寧酸
不傷腸胃不會睡不著

想及茶葉驗出農藥殘毒
衝擊愛泡茶的人們
台灣食安問題一波又一波
生活在食不安的恐懼中
有苦說不出的無助又無奈

讓生態保持自然平衡
開始友善種茶的茶農
新研製的台灣特色好茶
QR Code 可查生產履歷
通過歐盟嚴格檢驗
我尋得可以安心喝的紅烏龍茶

2016.6.15

翠峰

相約到翠峰茶區
找茶農體驗茶製程
學會和工人一樣採茶

友善種植的茶樹
在晨曦中閃爍綠光
接受陽光溫暖照拂
白雲在伸手可及處

山頭瞬間起霧
雲瀑直下千尺
緊緊抱住茶園
飄渺如仙境

厚實茶葉富含胺基酸
製成滋味飽滿氣韻舒活的
蜜香烏龍茶

附記：翠峰山頭這片友善種植的茶園，被小綠葉蟬吸吮，賴永富製
　　　茶師將其製成「蜜香烏龍茶」，是今年榮獲米其林三星的
　　　好茶。

2016.8.15

茶園生態

茶園生態他最瞭解
小綠葉蟬在嫩葉上吸吮
他不再噴農藥防治
讓茶樹自體癒合傷口

雜草在茶園生長
他不再使用除草劑
用手拔除雜草藤蔓
驚喜鳥類在樹下築巢

友善種植　已經
翻轉　茶園生態
回到無農藥時代

看見大自然最原始的
平衡機制啟動
力量生生不息

2017.12.15

製茶師

製茶師親力親為
掌握茶製程
從日光萎凋到室內萎凋
從機器攪拌炒菁

發酵的化學變化中
靠敏銳嗅覺與豐富歷練
聞茶香就知道
可以製成甘甜好茶

他最懂茶的生理
也懂愛茶人的心理
為了一杯好茶
忘了臉上滾動的汗水

2017.12.15

東方美人

茶葉條索鬆散　心芽白毫
外觀呈紅白黃綠褐五色

沖泡出琥珀色茶湯
初嚐有蜜香有果香
喉韻層次分明　甘潤醇厚
東方美人茶　不膨風

穿梭歷史時空
小綠葉蟬飛來飛去
停在茶樹嫩葉上
繼續吸吮

2013.10.15

紅玉

魚池鄉的紅茶達人
沖泡自製私房茶

道地台灣味
請遠來的詩人品飲

記憶裡的古早紅茶
喚醒舌尖　挑戰味蕾

紅玉讓我在午後
思緒重新啟動

2013.10.15

台灣高山烏龍

最愛紅泥小壺品春茶香
正是清明節前
手採一心兩葉
台灣高山烏龍

備生鐵壺煮山泉
水沸　鳥聲盈耳
呼朋引伴飛入
小壺內　茶葉在說話
互相展示初芽的鮮嫩

釋放茶香滿室
靜心品飲清亮茶湯
舌尖有點苦澀
入喉順滑韻無窮
啊！台灣絕品好茶

2013.10.15

文山包種

輕啜文山包種
茶香正當少女
每一個細胞都含情
神馳青春茶園

靈魂隨茶香飛翔
無茶　相思正濃
初戀的新鮮滋味
緊閉雙唇吞嚥生津

2015.10.15

蜜香紅茶

一杯茶分三口細品
茶湯在口腔圓舞
眼睛微閉用心感受
茶樹與小綠葉蟬和平共存
一期一會留在茶葉的回報

著涎蜜香紅茶強勁衝擊味蕾
舌尖瞬間由苦澀轉甘甜
花香蜜香果香層次豐富
愛茶人頻頻點頭
讚歎　無語　無聲

2015.10.15

霜降玉露

雲霧穿梭高山茶園
細心呵護厚實嫩葉
霜降後精製黃綠光澤茶乾

沖泡出嫩綠金黃透亮茶湯
細啜入口甘甜濃郁
頓覺茶質好入喉入心

內韻不絕　茶味的新極致
霜降玉露　台灣茶新極品

2015.10.15

炭焙烏龍

怎麼那樣深刻啊
連夢中也懷念的
茶，得上山尋找

發酵程度控制得剛好
茶質濃郁不苦澀
韻味層次豐富
全在口鼻空間

老師傅手工炭焙烏龍
醇厚如甘泉
喝到記憶裡的茶韻
夢中也會笑

2016.6.15

紅烏龍

八十五度C山泉水化開
百分之六十五發酵的
紅烏龍，茶師現泡

從嗅覺到味覺
喝完第一杯茶
特殊的紅烏龍茶韻
談話之間轉為甘醇

茶氣強如太平洋季風
積鬱的細胞開始甦醒
受困的神經獲得舒活

興奮的品茗心情
微波盪漾鹿野溪
千萬年的能量

2016.6.15

蜜香烏龍

詩人們尋訪翠峰茶區
茶師親泡蜜香烏龍
析出各種元素神祕混合
如蜜般滑順進入喉間

一杯好茶的特別底蘊
至今仍溫暖詩人們
沉澱成心靈詩篇

茶葉經過小綠葉蟬吸吮
捲曲變形的著涎葉片
精製成蜜香烏龍
出國比賽獲得米其林三星

盡得天時地利人和
製茶師用心製好茶
讓世界看見台灣

2018.2.15

一杯茶

一杯茶是舌尖上打滾的天池
——陳志良書家揮毫相贈

一杯茶
青年時喝
全身清泉奔流
啟發美好人生

一杯茶
壯年時喝
百般苦澀滋味
化作奮鬥勇氣

一杯茶
中年時喝
朗誦世界詩歌
禮讚愛與和平

一杯茶
老年時喝
人生淡淡回甘
留住許多回憶

一杯茶
千種滋味
在舌尖上打滾
詩留天地人間

2015.10

茶師

茶師，開始泡茶
掌握茶葉、水溫、時間
追求茶湯藝術
品味生活美學

不同種類的茶葉
選用不同的茶壺
感受不同的氛圍
辨別不同茶滋味

茶色，由濃轉淡
茶湯，由熱變冷
人生，一席茶
茶師，一卷書

2016.6.15

好茶在台灣

聞茶香　湯入喉間
身體感覺茶在導引
不著痕跡的振動
極特殊的新頻率

我問：這是那款茶

製茶師得意訴說
現在喝的是四季春
改以創新的製茶技術
今年唯一得到米其林三星

燈下　談茶山論茶水
三人跋涉一山又一山
一起慢慢品味獨步全球的
好茶在台灣

附記：2015年9月6日台Ａ茶賴維科先生邀我一起去南投茶博，會後，張三我製茶師邀我們到鹿谷他家，品味今年唯一得到米其林三星的好茶。夜宿鹿谷寫。

2016.8.15

茶境

慢慢喝　一杯茶又
一杯茶的時間裡
心隨茶自在

茶會心　心會茶
似有我　似無我
虛實相對　頓覺
時空　無限寬廣

杯空　留韻
放下　心　空

2016.8.15

茶韻催詩

壺中的凍頂烏龍茶
翻滾在雲霧之間
破空而入手捏茶杯
溫熱我的生活詩篇

被深厚茶韻催生的
是什麼樣的詩句
引繆斯飛進飛出
長繭的詩思已破了洞

如果飛出的是蝴蝶
外面的世界
一定要長滿鮮花
讓詩人可以流連駐足

如果飛出的是蜜蜂
外面的世界多風雨

隨時備好充足的蜜
讓詩人可以安心寫詩

讓茶韻昇華詩句
忙裡偷閒坐下來享受
喝一杯茶的幸福
寫一首詩的成就感

2017.2.15

試新茶

到茶山訪茶農，試新茶
注水入台灣柴燒壺
靜置一分鐘，等待
春茶醒來香氣乘雲霧

奉茶　一泡一杯
好茶　一期一會
茶香茶韻在鼻在口在心
天空澄淨心中無塵

2017.6.15

茶生活

茶生活是日常
不管工作雲淡日麗
或者壓力雨驟風狂

我一樣堅持
坐下來
泡壺茶
調適自己的心

茶湯順暢流出
化開外在環境激盪
心，復歸平靜。

意識到自己的心
只有自己可以安住
不隨喜怒哀樂波動
不隨時間長河流轉

2017.10.15

六龜山茶

六龜山茶蘊含
南台灣陽光雨露
成就特有山韻
茶滋味深入記憶

喬木茶樹藏在
國有地的雜木林中
太陽下閃著綠光
幼嫩茶葉稀少珍貴

採茶人在清明節前後
上山　尋找去年才認識的
茶樹　生長在寸步難行的
山溝旁有三棵　上去還有

製茶師熟記的製茶口訣
難以掌握野生山茶特性

試茶　改善　再改善
今年新製成的六龜山茶

喬木烏龍，微苦澀
還有隱士的高傲之氣
喬木紅茶，回甘快
留住君子的飽滿厚實

2019.6.15

港口茶

季節風強勁也吹不動
母本壓條繁殖的茶樹盤根
用生命緊緊抓住土地

抵抗海風的茶樹
跟著屏東的春天吶喊
你若來恆春　要喝一杯

原汁鹹味港口茶
加上海鹽調味
人生肯定淡淡回甘

2019.6.15

蜜香紅茶的原鄉

我謙卑跪在地上
相機以極低角度
如螞蟻的視域
仰望掃叭石柱
雄偉矗立所存在空間

偉大的創作者啊
以簡單線條開鑿
歷史的時間長河
為生存而奮鬥的座標
表現藝術的永恆

我俯身貼近茶園
以平視角度攝影
記錄花蓮北回歸線附近
在自然環境生長的茶葉
接受小綠葉蟬吸吮

葉片破相且著涎
茶農精製時有蜜香
命名：蜜香紅茶
的原鄉──花蓮瑞穗
掃叭石柱是見證者

2019.6.15

坪林茶區

喜見茶樹沐浴淨身
嫩綠茶葉在雨中
傾聽：人生是茶席
聚散隨緣永不止息

翡翠水庫上游賞景
淹沒區的民宅再也出不來
坪林茶區當下半遮
新景點千島湖全憑想像

老茶農賣茶的小舖
文山包種重現嫩綠
試喝看見茶湯
映入山色水光

淡香清雅點開了柔波
聞雷聲催發春芽
雨中詩意盎然的坪林

2019.6.15

在一碗茶的時間裡

捧著熱呼呼的一碗茶
多麼溫暖啊，像太陽
傳輸到心的深處
熱力瞬間通達全身
足以抵抗強烈寒流
重新開始，找回往昔
為理想而激發的戰鬥力

鳥隱藏枝椏間歌唱
肉眼雖然看不見
聽聲音可以辨識
是經常被關的台灣畫眉
鳥，正叫喚伴侶過來
共同抵抗強烈寒流

鳥聲不斷地叫喚
啊！是在提醒我吧

要隨時保持警覺
終止紛亂的訊息干擾
才不會被寒流凍僵
清醒看淡一切事情
快樂生活心安自在
享受鳥的自由歌唱
找回寫詩的興味

洋溢在古厝氛圍
詩的精靈微妙鑿開
腦海裡的意象
從潛藏的深層內裡
紛飛的詩句
躍出一行又一行
潦草抄寫在紙上
在一碗茶的時間裡

2019.4.15

天地茶席

南投茶葉博覽會
千人參加天地茶席
大家隨緣而坐
敘人生一席茶

相逢不必相識
茶師　以歡喜心
大家請坐　奉茶
請趁熱喝

台灣特色好茶
溫暖感情線
連接生命線
跨越智慧線

2019.6.15

人生茶席

人生茶席
要趁熱品飲
好茶淡淡香
甘甜生津

莫要等到
茶涼
人散
成為奠茶

人生恰是茶席
來
去
只一席茶時間

2019.10.15

找茶趣

茶人總是痴心
行走雲海之上
在台灣產茶的山區

品嚐清明節前手摘
一心兩葉春芽
心動的茶滋味
人生能找到幾回

乘想像的翅膀
心隨明月上茶山
快樂歡喜就在當下

2019.10.15

作者簡介

　　李昌憲，台南人，現居高雄市。曾參加森林詩社、綠地詩社、陽光小集、笠詩社。曾任職上市電子公司經理，創作以詩文、篆刻、陶藝、攝影為主。現為《笠詩刊》主編，高雄市第一社區大學篆刻老師，世界詩人運動組織（Movimiento Poetas del Mundo）會員。

　　1981年6月出版第一本詩集《加工區詩抄》，並於1982年獲「笠詩獎」。其他出版詩集《生態集》1993、《生產線上》1996、《仰觀星空》2005、《從青春到白髮》2005、《台灣詩人群像‧李昌憲詩集》2007、《台灣詩人選集‧李昌憲集》2010、《美的視界——慢遊大高雄詩攝影集》2014、《高雄詩情》2016、《愛河——漢英雙語詩集》2018。詩作〈期待曲〉詩句被選入【高雄市文學步道】；詩作〈加班〉、〈企業無情〉被選入【科大國文選】；及年度詩選、國內外之詩選集，被以英、日、韓、西、德、蒙等文字翻譯及介紹。

譯者簡介

Emily Anna Deasy

愛爾蘭科克大學亞洲語言學系對外漢語學碩士畢業。

西元1987年生。愛爾蘭籍。

曾居住台灣台北十五年,現居加拿大溫哥華。

加拿大卑詩省翻譯協會成員。

翻譯及同步翻譯經驗累積達十六年餘。

The Tea Session

of Life

Simply Tea Poems

Life
Starts from a cup of tea

The fragrance floats
The white clouds emerge
Tea-picking landscape
Hangs in the heart
Deeply poetic

Time
Like a Zen master seated

Tasting tea
Sweet brew
Good inspiration comes
Write down a poem
Ah! Simply tea poems

April 15, 2010

Tasting Tea

Brew a pot of good tea after coming home from work
Give an exit to the stress of work

The water tosses and turns between the tea and the pot
Emotions are smoothed out like the tea

All slowly   slowly
Slowly   slowly   settles

Taste the soul in the tea
A realm that blends into one

April 15, 2010

Maintaining the Teapot

Maintaining the teapot   talking about the universe
Thirty years and the true emotion is the same

Carefully stroking your skin
Every inch is love

Your face is full of rosy colour
My hair is a white crane flying in the snow

The fleeting of a lifetime brings a sigh
Only hope that time goes gently in the teapot

April 15, 2010

The Fragrance of Warm Tea

The fragrance of warm tea   this moment

The tea leaves wake up in the pot

The clouds that cover the tea mountain

Hide the tea leaves   to brew

Fragrance   swiftly fills this room

The fragrance of warm tea   this moment

The host and guest gather   linked by serendipity

Tea-lovers use five types of senses*

To taste the tea fragrance wafting in the white porcelain cup

The joy of each day being a good day

*Note: **Eyes:** vison- to watch the process of tea-making.
Ears: hearing- to listen to the instructions and adding their own experience, to interpret the tea brew.
Nose: smell- to smell and see if there is any strange smells from the tea leaves, and to smell the fragrance after brewing.
Tongue: taste- sweet, bitter, refreshing, smooth, aftertaste etc. according to individual taste.
Body: touch- lightly rubbing the tea leaves between the fingers, and if they are fragile it means they are fresh. For brewed tea leaves, you can tell if they are double-leaved and hand-picked, or picked with machinery.
The above explanation is just an example; by making the environment of tea-drinking (tea-drinking seats, utensils, leaves etc.) into an art to be appreciated, as a practice, according to individual needs, as long as people like it.

October 15, 2013

Life

After retirement a slow realization

That life is calm and without contention

No pressure from work that can be aroused

Feel the freedom and happiness with your heart

Free time after unrestricted creating

Tasting tea and then forgetting it, and then silence

February 15, 2015

Magnolia Tea Aroma

Smelling the tea aromas while driving miles in their hundreds

Checking in to a hostel run by tea farmers

Perched upon the mountaintop with far-reaching views

We look across the fertile Lanyang Plain

Let the wind iron out the pressure that has built up

After enjoying a dinner with flavours full of character

The tea farmers invite us to try a new tea

As if we are walking out from a cloud of mist

The brew of Magnolia tea is light and refreshing

Drink with a calm heart in these surroundings

Our host takes out the first prize tea

The aroma confronts the nose and enters the lungs

The brew moistens the throat and surrenders the sweetness

All homes of Lanyang Plain in their tens of thousands

Come and taste the Magnolia tea aroma

October 15, 2013

To Maokong in Search of Iron Guanyin

Wanting to taste authentic Iron Guanyin from Muzha

More than ten years ago my daughter accompanied me, following
     the description in a book

To go to Maokong in search of the Iron Guanyin contest tea

Award-winning tea just brought home and brewed by an expert

Dark amber clear tea

The aroma of ripened fruit is too strong to dissipate

The roasted scent dances on the tip of the tongue

He said: you have to leave it be for a while

Wait for the roasted scent to retreat in full

Then this kind of tea will be more sweet and pure

Zhang tea farmers brought the shoots of Iron Guanyin tea

From Anxi and across the Black Ditch* to plant in the Muzha area

The tea tree is green every year　The stream from the Maokong

    teapot runs and runs

It is here that the tea-making skills of the Iron Guanyin passes from

    generation to generation

October 15, 2013

* The Black Ditch here references the Taiwan Straight

Jade Lake

Walking in the tea garden and the bamboo forest

Looking closely at the tea trees to see the new shoots emerging

Looking far to see the Taiwan mountains competing for height

What a lovely portrait of the tea mountain

The path is crooked   walk to the trigonometrical station of Dajian
    Mountain

From clear skies to cloudy

And between breaths   the mountain rain comes

Sending everyone retreating right away

I hope the next rain brings relief from the summer heat

It must be fortunate to be in the rain with the tea trees

My thoughts suspend above the clouds

The lines of poetry flip and fly as they stroll among the mountains

The guest asks: why is there no lake at Jade Lake

The owner replies: the clouds and fog are the lake

As you look outside right now

It is up to you to imagine whether that is a lake or an ocean

The owner brews his own good tea

Inviting everyone to calm their heart and appreciate it

With a kind heart loving

Truly appreciating the good mountains and good water of Taiwan

October 15, 2013

Making Tea on the Mountain

Try tea-making for yourself
Let the mountain air steam your whole body
Let your sweat soak your body through

Roll and twist the newly-picked tea leaves evenly
Break it up and roll it again
Let it ferment in the tea-making room

Wait the time   sit with legs crossed like a Zen master
The tea trees softly enter into the room of my heart
And the fog clouds follow in

When the fermenting reaches the expected point
It is dried into a deep brown red oolong
The tea is singing   we listen carefully

October 15, 2015

Travels in Search of Red Oolong

Luye Highland is covered in the soft spring rain
The owner of Housheng tea gardens details
The process of making red oolong

With newly-picked double-leaf oolong tea leaves
Wilting and stirring again and again
A special roasting technology
Retaining ingredients that are good for the drinker
Reducing caffeine tannins
Preventing harm to the stomach as well as sleepless nights

To think of pesticides being found in tea leaves
Shocking those who love to brew tea
Wave after wave of food safety issues in Taiwan
Living in fear of eating something unsafe
Helplessness and despair that is hard to articulate

May the ecosystem maintain its natural balance

The tea farmer who grows tea with a kind heart

Newly developed Taiwanese specialty tea

With production history traceable via QR code

Having passed strict EU inspections

I have found the red oolong that I can drink with peace.

June 15, 2016

Cueifong

We meet at the Cueifong tea region
Experiencing the tea-making process with tea farmers
Learning to pick tea like the workers

Tea trees planted in a friendly way
Glistening green in the morning light
Accept the warmth of the sun
The clouds are at your fingertips

Fog comes to the hilltops suddenly
A waterfall of cloud that goes down a thousand feet
Hold on tightly to the tea garden
It is ethereal

Strong tea leaves rich in amino acids
Made into a full-bodied and soothing
Honey oolong tea

Note: this tea garden on the Cuifeng hilltops, where the leaves are
      sucked by tea green leafhoppers, has been made into 'Honey
      Oolong Tea' by tea maker Yongfu Lai. This tea has been
      awarded three Michelin stars this year.

August 15, 2016

Tea Garden Ecology

Tea garden ecology, he knows best

As the tea green leafhopper sucks on young leaves

He no longer sprays pesticides

But lets the tea tree heal its own wounds

Weeds grow in the tea gardens

He no longer uses herbicides

He removes the weed vines by hand

And is surprised to see the birds nesting under the tree

Friendly planting   has

Flipped   the tea garden ecology

Back to the era of no pesticide use

See nature's most original

Balance mechanism start up

The power goes on forever

December 15, 2017

Tea Maker

The personal touch of the tea maker

Mastering the tea-making process

From the dwindling sunlight it is brought in to dwindle

Roasted as it is stirred in the machine

In the chemical process of fermentation

Relying on a keen sense of smell and rich experience

By the scent of the tea I will know

It can be made into a fine sweet tea

He knows the physiology of tea

And understands the minds of tea-lovers

For a good cup of tea

He forgets the sweat that is rolling down his face

December 15, 2017

Oriental Beauty

Tea leaves in loose strips   white hearts
Five-coloured exterior, red, white, yellow, green and brown

Brews an amber coloured tea
The first taste is of honey and of fruit
Clear layers in the throat sweet and mellow
Oriental beauty tea   lives up to its name

Go through the space and time of history
Green leaf-hoppers fly here and there
They stop on the young leaf of a tea tree
And continue to taste

October 15, 2013

Red Jade

Black tea masters in Yuchi Township
Brewing their own special tea

An authentic Taiwanese taste
May the poet who comes from afar taste and enjoy

Ancient black tea in my memory
Awakens the tip of the tongue   challenging my taste buds

Red Jade in the afternoon
Restarts my thoughts

October 15, 2013

Taiwan High Mountain Oolong

Love to taste the spring tea scent in a small red clay pot

Just before Ching Ming Festival

Hand-picked double-leaf with one heart

Taiwan high mountain oolong

Prepare the iron pot to boil the mountain spring water

The water boils   birdsong comes to the ear

Gathering friends it flies inside

In the small pot   the tea leaves are speaking

Showing each other the fresh tenderness of the first bud

The scent of tea releases and fills the room

Calm the heart and taste the bright clear brew

Some bitterness at the tip of the tongue

It goes down the throat with infinite smoothness

Ah! The finest tea of Taiwan

October 15, 2013

Wenshan Pouchong

Lightly sip Wenshan Pouchong

The tea scent is a young girl

Every cell holds emotion

Thinking of the tea garden of youth

The soul flies with the tea

No tea   missing one another deeply

The fresh new taste of a first love

Close lips tightly and swallow it down

October 15, 2015

Honey Black Tea

Taste a cup of tea in three mouthfuls

The brew dances round in the mouth

Lightly close the eyes and feel

The peaceful coexistence of the tea trees and the green leaf-hoppers

And each one-time reward that stays in the tea leaves

The taste of Honey Black Tea impacts the taste buds strongly

A swift turn from bitter to sweet on the tip of the tongue

Floral, honey, fruity, rich layers

Tea lovers nod, one after the other

Admiration speechless without a sound

October 15, 2015

Frosted Jade Drop

The fog crosses the high mountain tea gardens
The carefully cared for thick leaves
Dried tea made after the frost has a yellow-green sheen

Brewing green and golden translucent tea
Small sips that turn sweet as they enter the mouth
The quality of the fine tea can be felt in the throat and the heart

An inner rhythm that does not end   A new pinnacle for tea scent
Frosted Jade Drop A new best for Taiwan tea

October 15, 2015

Charcoal Roasted Oolong

How is it so profound

I miss it even in my dreams

Tea, must go to the mountains to seek

The fermentation is controlled just right

The tea is rich and not bitter

Rich layers of flavour

All in the nose and mouth

The old master handcrafts charcoal roasted oolong

Mellow as a sweet spring

Drink the tea in my memories

And even in my dreams, I laugh

June 15, 2016

Red Oolong

Spread out in eighty-five degree Celsius mountain spring water
65 percent fermented
Red oolong, freshly brewed by the tea master

From smell to taste
Drink up the first cup of tea
Unique taste of red oolong tea
Turns sweet between conversations

The tea scent is as strong as the Pacific monsoon
The stagnant cells began to wake
The trapped nerves get some relief

Excited mood to taste the tea
Light ripples flow in Luye Creek
Energy from millions of years

June 15, 2016

Honey Oolong

Poets visit the Cuifeng Tea Region

The tea master brews honey oolong

Separates various elements into a mysterious mixture

Goes down the throat smooth as honey

A special recipe for a good cup of tea

That still warms the poets to this day

And settles to form a spiritual poem

The tea leaves are sucked on by the green leaf-hoppers

The leaves are curled and reshaped

Refined into honey oolong

That won a Michelin star competing abroad

With all the right conditions

The tea master works hard to make good tea

Making Taiwan seen in the eyes of the world

February 15, 2018

A Cup of Tea

A cup of tea is Heaven Lake rolling on the tip of the tongue
Given by the brush of Zhi-liang Chen

A cup of tea
Drank during one's youth
Clear springs run through the body
Inspiring a beautiful life

A cup of tea
Drank during one's prime
All kinds of bitter tastes
Develop into the courage to fight

A cup of tea
Drank during one's mid-life
Recite the poetry of the world
In praise of love and peace

A cup of tea

Drank during old age

Life brings a faint sweet aftertaste

Holding onto many memories

A cup of tea

A thousand tastes

Rolling on the tip of the tongue

Poetry lives on forever

October, 2015

Tea Masters

Tea masters, begin to brew the tea

Managing the tea leaves, water temperature, and time

Pursuing the art of the brew

Tasting the esthetics of life

Different types of tea leaves

Call for the choice of different pots

A different ambiance

To discern the tastes of the different teas

The colour of the tea turns from dark to light

The brew goes from hot to cold

Life, a cup of tea

Tea masters, a book

June 15, 2016

Good Tea is in Taiwan

Smell the tea aroma   the brew goes down the throat

The body feels the guidance of the tea

A vibration that leaves no trace

A new frequency that is extremely special

I ask: which type of tea is this

The tea-making master happily says

That I am drinking Four Seasons Spring

That is modified with innovative tea-making skills

The only to get a Michelin star this year

Under the light   talking all about tea

Three people rambling over one mountain after another

Slowly tasting that which is special all over the world

Good tea is in Taiwan

August 15, 2016

Tea Ambiance

Drink slowly a cup of tea and
The time it takes to drink another cup
The heart is freed along with the tea

The tea meets the heart   the heart meets the tea
As if I was there   as if I was not there at all
False and true come head-to-head   realization
Time and space   are infinitely broad

Cup is empty   leaves the aftertaste
Put it down   heart   emptiness

August 15, 2016

Poem-prompting Tea

The Tung-ting oolong tea in the pot
Rolls between the mist and cloud
A hand breaks through and clutches the cup
Warming the poems of my life

Which kind of poetry lines
Will the deep aftertaste prompt to life
Muses flies in and out
Breaking a hole in the calloused train of thought

If it is a butterfly that flies out
The outside world
Must be growing full of fresh flowers
To stop the poet in wonderment

If a honey bee flies out
The world outside will be windy and rainy

Always prepared with enough honey
For the poet to write peacefully

Let the aftertaste evaporate into lines of poetry
And steal a moment of enjoyment amid the busyness
Take a drink of the happiness of tea
The sense of accomplishment from writing a poem

February 15, 2017

Trying New Tea

Visiting the tea farmers on the tea mountain, trying new tea

Channel the water into the Taiwan firewood teapot

Leave it for one minute, waiting

Spring tea awakens and the aroma rides the mist and cloud

Offer the tea a cup per brew

Good tea each meeting is a once-in-a-lifetime

The aroma and aftertaste of the tea stays in the nose, mouth and heart

The sky is clear and the heart is clean

June 15, 2017

Tea life

Tea life is everyday
Whether work is sunny clear skies
Or stress like strong wind and rain

I persist regardless
Sitting down
Brewing a pot of tea
Settling my heart

The brew flows out smoothly
Spreading through the surrounding ripples
My heart, returns to calm

I realise that only I can calm
My own heart
Not letting it shift with sorrow or joy
Not changing with time like a river

October 15, 2017

Liouguei Mountain Tea

Liouguei mountain tea contains
Rain and sunshine from southern Taiwan
A unique mountain taste
Which goes deep into the memory

Arbor tea tree hidden in
The woods within the state-owned land
Green light sparkles under the sun
Young tea leaves are rare and precious

Around the time of the Ching Ming Festival, tea-pickers
Go up the mountain looking for what they knew just last year
Tea trees growing in the dense
Three trees next to the ravine more as you go up

The tea-makers have memorized their tea-making lines
The characteristics of the wild mountain tea are difficult to grasp

Try the tea improve it then improve it again
Liouguei mountain tea newly made this year

Arbor oolong, slightly bitter
With a hermit's air of pride
Arbor black tea, the sweetness comes swiftly
Retaining the all-roundedness of the gentleman

June 15, 2019

Port Tea

Strong seasonal winds can't blow

Tea tree roots that grow from layering

Grasping the land with life

Tea tree against the sea breeze

Follow the spring scream of Shandong

If you come to Hengchun you must have a cup

Salty port tea

Seasoned with Shanghai salt

Life must surely have a faint aftertaste

June 15, 2019

The Hometown of Honey Black Tea

I humbly kneel on the ground
With the camera at a very low angle
As if from the viewpoint of the ant
Gazing up at the Saoba stone pillars
At the majestic space

Great creator
Carved out with simple lines
The long river of history
The marker of struggle for survival
To show how art is eternal

I stand against and lean over the tea garden
Taking photos at a level angle
In Hualien, near the Tropic of Cancer
I record the tea leaves that grow in a natural environment
With the sucking of leaf-hoppers

The leaves are bitten and broken

Smelling like honey as the tea farmers refine

Named: Honey Black Tea

Hometown - Hualien Ruisui

The Saoba pillars are the witnesses

June 15, 2019

Pinglin Tea District

With joy I see the tea tree bathing

The tender green tea leaves in the rain

Listen: life is a round of tea

Gathering endlessly

Sightseeing over Feicui Dam

The homes in the flooded area are no more

Half covered by Pinglin tea district

The new spot Qiandao Lake is all imagination

An old tea farmer's stall

Green leaves are important for Wenshan Baozhong tea

Try it and see how the brew

Reflects the mountains and water

The light fragrance elegantly opens the soft waves

The sound of thunder prompts the new spring shoots

The poetic Pinglin in the rain

June 15, 2019

In the Time It Takes to Have a Cup of Tea

Holding a steaming hot cup of tea

How warm it is, like the sun

Sending to the depths of the heart

Heat instantly reaches the whole body

Enough to fight the strong cold current

Start over, find the past

The power to fight for ideals

The birds hide in the branches and sing

Even though they are not seen

You can make out from their sound

That they are the often-trapped Taiwanese thrush

Calling for a mate to come and fight the strong cold current together

The call of the birds is constant!

It is reminding me

To be always alert

Put an end to the chaotic interfering messages

So as to not be frozen by the cold current

Stay awake and take things lightly

Happy, peaceful, and carefree life

Enjoy the free singing of the birds

Find again interest in writing poems

Surrounded by ancient atmosphere

The poetry elves are chiselling away

Imagery in the mind

From the hidden deep inside

Flying verses

Jumping out one line after another

Scribbled on paper

In the time it takes to have a cup of tea

April 15, 2019

Heaven and Earth Tea Sessions

Nantou Tea Expo

Thousands of people attend the heaven and earth tea sessions

Everyone freely takes a place

A narrative of the tea of life

No need to know each other in order to meet

Tea master with a joyful heart

Please take a seat tea is served

Please drink up while hot

Taiwan's specialty good tea

Warms the heart line

Connects the life line

Steps over the wisdom line

June 15, 2019

The Tea Session of Life

The tea session of life

Drink up while hot

The light scent of good tea

Sweet and soothing

Do not wait until

The tea has cooled

The people gone

And it becomes settled tea

Life is a tea session

Comes

Goes

In just the time it takes for a session of tea

October 15, 2019

The Interest in Tea

Tea-lovers are always obsessed

Walking above the sea and clouds

In the tea-making mountain regions of Taiwan

Taste the double-leafed, single hearted tea leaf

Hand-picked before Ching Ming Festival

The moving taste of the tea

How many times can it be found in life

Fly on the wings of imagination

The heart goes up the tea mountain along with the clear moon

Happiness and joy are in the moment

October 15, 2019

About the Author

Lee Chang-hsien was born in Tainan and is currently living in Kaohsiung City. He has previously participated in Forest Poetry Society, Green Poetry Society, Little Sunshine Collection, and Li Poetry Society. He has worked as a manager at a listed electronics company. His creative works mainly lie in poetry, seal carving, pottery, and photography. He is currently the editor-in-chief of Li Poetry Journal and a seal carving teacher at the Kaohsiung First Community University. He is also the member of Movimiento Poetas del Mundo.

In June 1981, he published his first collection of poetry, *Poems of the Processing Zone*, and in 1982 he won the Li Poetry Award. Other poetry collections published include *Ecology Collection* (1993), *On the Production Line* (1996), *Looking Up at the Starry Skies* (2005), *From Youth to Grey Hair* (2005), *Portraits of Taiwanese Poets-The* Lee Chang-hsien *Poetry Anthology*

(2007), *Selected Works of a Taiwanese Poet- The* Lee Chang-hsien *Collection* (2010), *A Vision of Beauty- Slow Travel in Greater Kaohsiung Poetry and Photography Collection* (2014), *Poetics of Kaohsiung* (2016).Love River-- Chinese-English (2018) Lines from his poem *Song of Expectation* was selected into the Kaohsiung City Literature Trail; his poems *Overtime* and *Ruthless Enterprises* were selected in *Selected Works of Chinese Literature for Universities of Technology*; his work is published in annual poetry selections, national and international poetry collections, and has been translated and introduced in English, Japanese, Korean, Spain, German and Mongolian.

About the Translator

Emily Anna Deasy was born in Ireland in 1987, and has almost sixteen years of translation and interpreting experience. Emily spent fifteen years of her live living in Taipei, Taiwan. She received her master's degree in TCSOL (Teaching Chinese to Speakers of Other Languages) from University College Cork, Ireland, and is a member of the Society of Translators and Interpreters of BC, Canada, where she currently resides.

CONTENTS

語言文學類　PG2409　台灣詩叢10

人生茶席：台灣茶詩
The Tea Session of Life：
The poems of Taiwanese Tea
——李昌憲漢英雙語詩集

作　　　者 / 李昌憲（Lee Chang-hsien）
譯　　　者 / 戴茉莉（Emily Anna Deasy）
叢 書 策 劃 / 李魁賢（Lee Kuei-shien）
責 任 編 輯 / 林昕平、陳彥儒
圖 文 排 版 / 周好靜
封 面 設 計 / 劉肇昇

發 　行 　人 / 宋政坤
法 律 顧 問 / 毛國樑　律師
出 版 發 行 / 秀威資訊科技股份有限公司
　　　　　　114台北市內湖區瑞光路76巷65號1樓
　　　　　　電話：+886-2-2796-3638　傳真：+886-2-2796-1377
　　　　　　http://www.showwe.com.tw
劃 撥 帳 號 / 19563868　戶名：秀威資訊科技股份有限公司
　　　　　　讀者服務信箱：service@showwe.com.tw
展 售 門 市 / 國家書店（松江門市）
　　　　　　104台北市中山區松江路209號1樓
　　　　　　電話：+886-2-2518-0207　傳真：+886-2-2518-0778
網 路 訂 購 / 秀威網路書店：https://store.showwe.tw
　　　　　　國家網路書店：https://www.govbooks.com.tw

2020年8月　BOD一版
定價：200元
版權所有　翻印必究
本書如有缺頁、破損或裝訂錯誤，請寄回更換

國家圖書館出版品預行編目

人生茶席：台灣茶詩: 李昌憲漢英雙語詩集 /
李昌憲著. 戴茉莉譯 -- 一版. -- 臺北市：
秀威資訊科技, 2020.08
　　面；　公分. -- (語言文學類)(台灣詩叢；10)
中英對照
BOD版
ISBN 978-986-326-817-8(平裝)

863.51　　　　　　　　　　　　109006684

讀者回函卡

感謝您購買本書，為提升服務品質，請填妥以下資料，將讀者回函卡直接寄回或傳真本公司，收到您的寶貴意見後，我們會收藏記錄及檢討，謝謝！如您需要了解本公司最新出版書目、購書優惠或企劃活動，歡迎您上網查詢或下載相關資料：http:// www.showwe.com.tw

您購買的書名：_____

出生日期：_____年_____月_____日

學歷：□高中 (含) 以下　　□大專　　□研究所 (含) 以上

職業：□製造業　□金融業　□資訊業　□軍警　□傳播業　□自由業
　　　□服務業　□公務員　□教職　　□學生　□家管　　□其它_____

購書地點：□網路書店　□實體書店　□書展　□郵購　□贈閱　□其他

您從何得知本書的消息？

　□網路書店　□實體書店　□網路搜尋　□電子報　□書訊　□雜誌

　□傳播媒體　□親友推薦　□網站推薦　□部落格　□其他_____

您對本書的評價：(請填代號　1.非常滿意　2.滿意　3.尚可　4.再改進)

　封面設計____　版面編排____　內容____　文／譯筆____　價格____

讀完書後您覺得：

　□很有收穫　□有收穫　□收穫不多　□沒收穫

對我們的建議：_____

_____

_____

_____

11466
台北市內湖區瑞光路 76 巷 65 號 1 樓

秀威資訊科技股份有限公司　　　收

BOD 數位出版事業部

....

（請沿線對折寄回，謝謝！）

姓　　名：＿＿＿＿＿＿＿＿＿　年齡：＿＿＿＿＿　性別：□女　□男

郵遞區號：□□□□□

地　　址：＿＿＿＿＿＿＿＿＿＿＿＿＿＿＿＿＿＿＿＿＿＿＿＿＿

聯絡電話：(日) ＿＿＿＿＿＿＿＿＿＿　(夜) ＿＿＿＿＿＿＿＿＿＿

E-mail：＿＿＿＿＿＿＿＿＿＿＿＿＿＿＿＿＿＿＿＿＿＿＿＿＿